HOW DOES IT WORK?

SOLAR PANELS

by Mari Schuh

pogo

Ideas for Parents and Teachers

Pogo Books let children practice reading informational text while introducing them to nonfiction features such as headings, labels, sidebars, maps, and diagrams, as well as a table of contents, glossary, and index.

Carefully leveled text with a strong photo match offers early fluent readers the support they need to succeed.

Before Reading

- "Walk" through the book and point out the various nonfiction features. Ask the student what purpose each feature serves.
- Look at the glossary together. Read and discuss the words.

Read the Book

- Have the child read the book independently.
- Invite him or her to list questions that arise from reading.

After Reading

- Discuss the child's questions. Talk about how he or she might find answers to those questions.
- Prompt the child to think more. Ask: Have you ever seen a solar panel? Where was it? What do you think it was helping power?

Pogo Books are published by Jump!
5357 Penn Avenue South
Minneapolis, MN 55419
www.jumplibrary.com

Library of Congress Cataloging-in-Publication Data

Names: Schuh, Mari C., 1975- author.
Title: Solar panels / by Mari Schuh.
Description: Minneapolis, MN: Jump!, Inc., 2021.
Series: How does it work?
Includes index. | Audience: Ages 7-10
Identifiers: LCCN 2020029537 (print)
LCCN 2020029538 (ebook)
ISBN 9781645277866 (hardcover)
ISBN 9781645277873 (paperback)
ISBN 9781645277880 (ebook)
Subjects: LCSH: Solar energy—Juvenile literature.
Classification: LCC TJ810.3 .S34 2021 (print)
LCC TJ810.3 (ebook) | DDC 621.31/244–dc23
LC record available at https://lccn.loc.gov/2020029537
LC ebook record available at https://lccn.loc.gov/2020029538

Editor: Eliza Leahy
Designer: Molly Ballanger

Photo Credits: magann/iStock, cover; Andrey_Popov/Shutterstock, 1; vilax/Shutterstock, 3; PRASANNAPIX/Shutterstock, 4 (left); Pormezz/Shutterstock, 4 (right); Juergen Faelchle/Shutterstock, 5; Visoot Uthairam/Dreamstime, 6-7; Goga Shutter/Shutterstock, 8; Dewald Kirsten/Shutterstock, 9; Education Images/Getty, 10-11; Aleksandar Mijatovic/Shutterstock, 12; marieclaudelemay/iStock, 12-13; Transtock/SuperStock, 14; diy13/Shutterstock, 15; Francisco Solipa/Dreamstime, 16-17; VCG/Getty, 18-19; Flamingo Images/Shutterstock, 20-21; Adem Demir/Shutterstock, 23.

Printed in the United States of America at Corporate Graphics in North Mankato, Minnesota.

TABLE OF CONTENTS

CHAPTER 1

WHAT ARE SOLAR PANELS?

Electricity is a kind of energy. We use it in homes and buildings. Lights, TVs, and **appliances** all use it.

Solar panels are one way to make electricity. How? They use the power of the sun!

Scientists have been working on **solar energy** since the 1800s. They keep finding ways to improve it. How? It is becoming more **efficient**. It is getting cheaper, too. People use it more and more.

Solar panels have **solar cells**. Frames connect them. They collect sunlight. They turn it into electricity. Let's find out how!

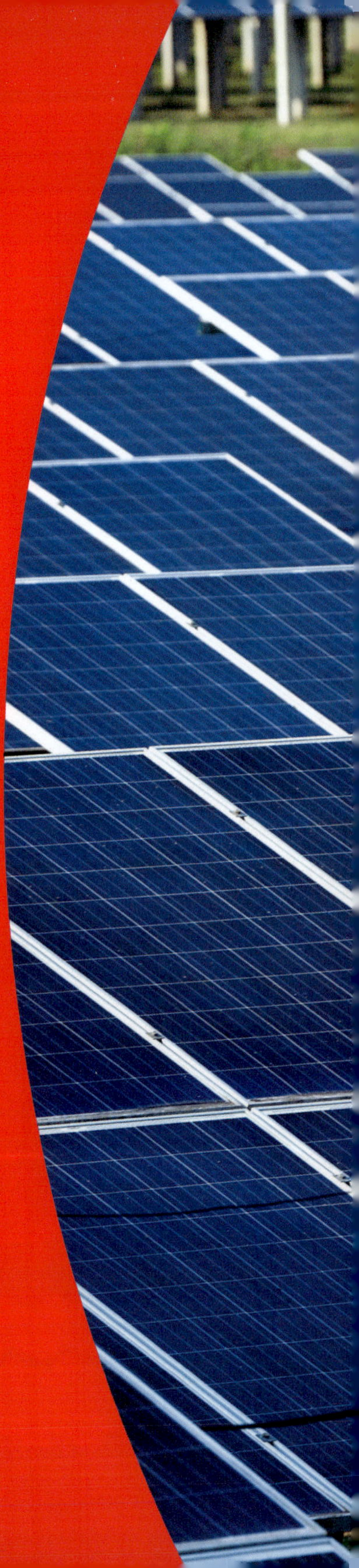

DID YOU KNOW?

In 2015 and 2016, a pilot flew a plane around the world. The plane made history. Why? Solar cells covered it. It used only energy from the sun.

frame

CHAPTER 2

HOW THEY WORK

Each solar cell has two layers. They are made of **silicon**. The silicon **absorbs** sunlight. Each cell has a coating, too. Why? It helps the cell absorb more sunlight.

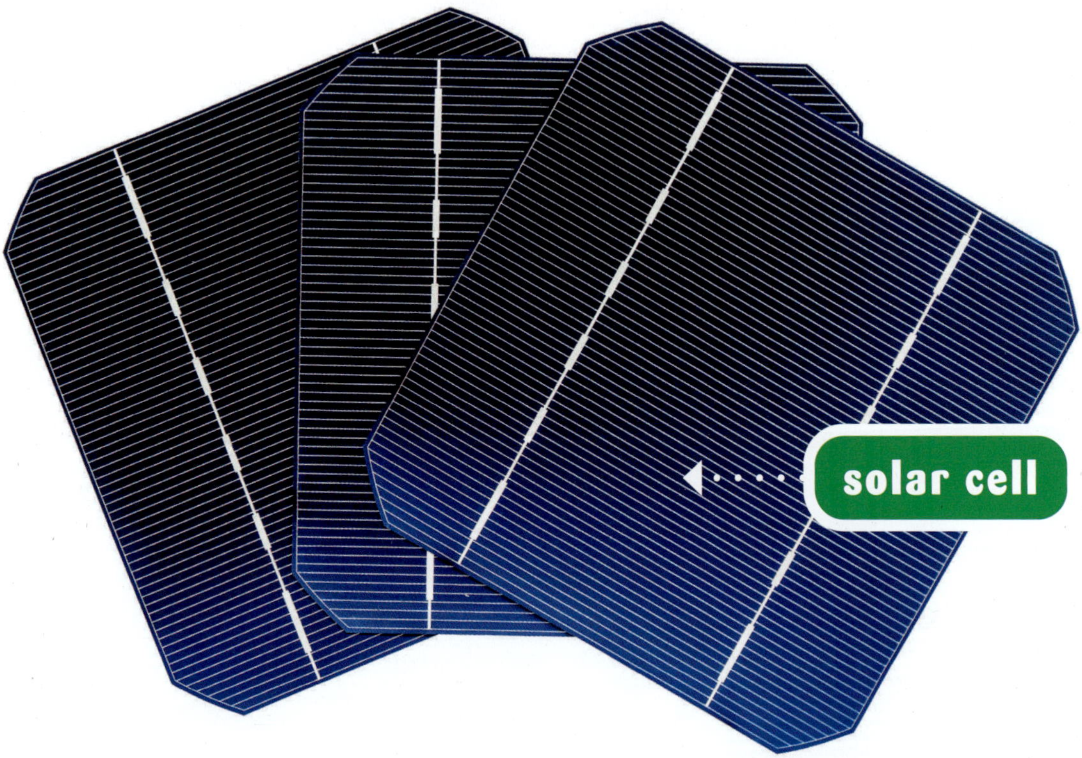

Look closely. The surface of each cell has metal strips. The bottom layer of each cell is metal, too. What does the metal do? It provides paths for **electrons**. **Particles** of light can hit a cell with lots of energy. This knocks electrons loose from their **atoms**. The electrons move. This makes an **electric current**.

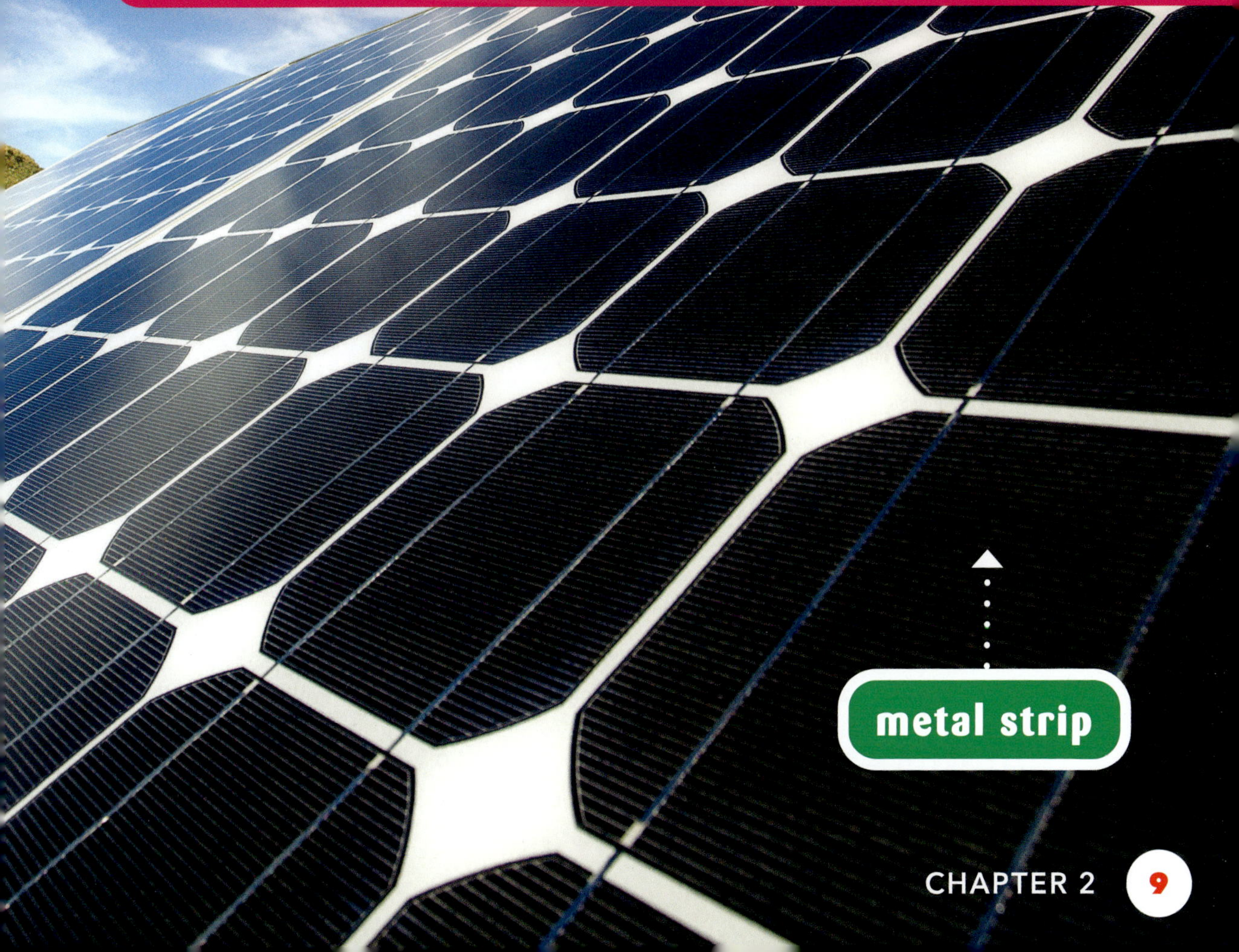

Where does the current go? It travels through wires. It goes to an inverter. The inverter changes the current. It turns it into electricity we can use.

Circuit breakers keep us safe. **Fuses** do, too. How? They stop the current if the wires get too hot. This can happen if too many appliances are being used.

TAKE A LOOK!

How do solar panels make electricity? Take a look!

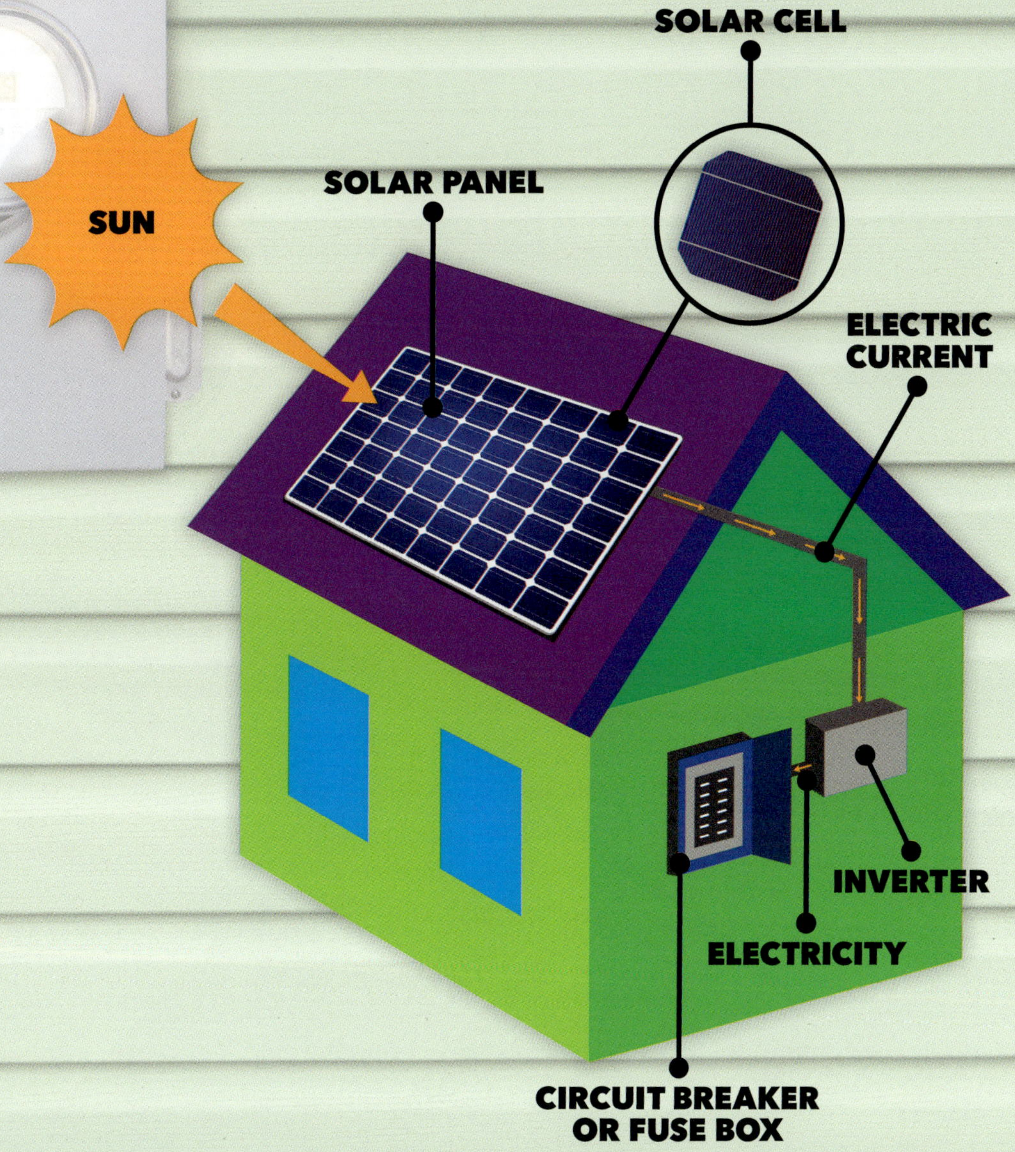

Solar collectors also absorb sunlight. But they are different from solar panels. How? They do not make electricity. They have pipes inside them. The sun's energy heats the pipes. They carry air or water. The air or water warms up. People can use it.

CHAPTER 3

SOLAR PANELS IN ACTION

Many solar panels are found on the roofs of buildings. They can also power parking meters, boats, and cars.

Sunlight can power tiny devices, too. Like what? It can power watches and calculators. It can also power phone chargers.

solar park

Solar parks are areas with many solar panels. They make a lot of energy! But land has to be cleared for them. This can mean less space for wildlife.

DID YOU KNOW?

There are other challenges to using solar panels. Like what? They are expensive. If it is cloudy, they do not make much power. They do not work at night.

Scientists find more ways to use solar panels. More roads and highways might have solar panels on them in the future. Where else might we use them?

solar highway

There are many benefits of using solar panels. Sunlight is free. It does not run out. Solar energy does not make pollution. It does not use **fossil fuels**, such as coal, oil, and natural gas. These can run out. They can pollute the air. Using them can make Earth warmer.

DID YOU KNOW?

You can use the power of the sun without solar panels. How? It is simple! On a cold day, open your curtains. Sunlight will shine through the windows. It will help warm your home!

ACTIVITIES & TOOLS

TRY THIS!

MAKE SUN TEA

Solar collectors use sunlight to heat air and water. You can use sunlight to heat water to make tea!

What You Need:

- clear glass jar
- teapot or container you can't see through
- water
- 4 to 6 tea bags
- thermometer
- pen or pencil
- notebook

1. **Start in the morning. Fill the jar and teapot mostly full of cold water. Add four to six tea bags to each container. Tightly close the jar's lid.**
2. **Put the jar and teapot in the sun. Try a windowsill or driveway.**
3. **Every hour, make sure the containers are still in the sun. Put a thermometer in the containers. Write the temperatures in a notebook.**
4. **If it is a hot, sunny day, the tea might be ready in two or three hours. If it's a cool, cloudy day, it could take about six hours. When the tea is done, compare the temperatures. Taste the tea in each container. Do they taste the same? Do they look the same? If not, why do you think that is?**

GLOSSARY

absorbs: Soaks up or takes in.

appliances: Machines created to do certain jobs; toasters, washing machines, and hair dryers are appliances.

atoms: The smallest building blocks of everything in the world.

circuit breakers: Switches that stop the flow of electric current in a circuit if it gets too strong.

efficient: Using less energy to perform a task.

electric current: A flow of electricity.

electricity: A form of energy that can be used to make light, heat, and motion.

electrons: The smallest particles within atoms.

fossil fuels: Fuels, such as coal, oil, and natural gas, that are formed in the earth from dead plants or animals.

fuses: Devices that stop the flow of electric current in a circuit if it gets too strong.

particles: Very small pieces of something.

silicon: An element found in Earth's crust that is often used in electronic devices.

solar cells: Devices that change the sun's light energy into electricity.

solar energy: Energy from the sun that is changed into electricity or heat.

solar parks: Large numbers of solar panels grouped together to produce solar energy; solar parks are also called solar farms or solar power stations.

INDEX

TO LEARN MORE

Finding more information is as easy as 1, 2, 3.

1. Go to www.factsurfer.com
2. Enter "solarpanels" into the search box.
3. Choose your book to see a list of websites.

FACT SURFER